Henry and Mudge
AND THE
Snowman Plan

The Nineteenth Book of Their Adventures

Story by Cynthia Rylant
Pictures by Suçie Stevenson

Ready-to-Read
Aladdin Paperbacks
New York London Toronto Sydney Singapore

For Samantha J. Wills—CR

For Benjamin Brown especially, and also for Joshua and Dennis Brown, and for Amy van der Clock Brown—SS

THE HENRY AND MUDGE BOOKS

First Aladdin Paperbacks Edition October 2000

Text copyright © 1999 by Cynthia Rylant
Illustrations copyright © 1999 by Suçie Stevenson

Aladdin Paperbacks
An imprint of Simon & Schuster
Children's Publishing Division
1230 Avenue of the Americas
New York, NY 10020

Also available in a Simon & Schuster Books for Young Readers edition.

The text for this book was set in 18-point Goudy.
The illustrations were rendered in pen-and-ink and watercolor.

Printed and bound in the United States of America

20 19 18

The Library of Congress has cataloged the hardcover edition as follows:

Rylant, Cynthia.
Henry and Mudge and the snowman plan : the nineteenth book of their adventures / story by
Cynthia Rylant ; pictures by Suçie Stevenson.
p.   cm. — (The Henry and Mudge books)
Summary: Henry, his dog Mudge, and his father enter a snowman-building contest at the local
park and win third place.
ISBN 0-689-81169-1 (hc.)
[Snowmen—Fiction. 2. Contests—Fiction. 3. Fathers and sons—Fiction. 4. Dogs—Fiction.]
I. Stevenson, Suçie, ill. II. Title III. Series: Rylant, Cynthia. Henry and Mudge books.
PZ7.R982Heap 1999
[E]—dc21
98-7042
ISBN 0-689-83449-7 (ISBN-13: 978-0-689-83449-3) (Aladdin pbk.)
0310 LAK

Contents

Contest!

On a snowy day in January,
Henry and Henry's big dog Mudge
saw a sign in a store window.
It said SNOWMAN CONTEST,
SATURDAY AT THE PARK.

"A snowman contest!"
said Henry. "Wow!"
Mudge wagged his tail.
He always wagged his tail
when Henry said, "Wow."
It meant excitement.

And sometimes it meant
dessert!
Henry ran home
to tell his father.

Henry's father was in the
basement, painting a chair.
He had green paint on his
hair, across his nose,
and in his mustache.

"Guess what, Dad?" said Henry.

(Mudge was looking for a

special old boot.)

"What?" asked Henry's father.

He wiped some paint across his chin.

"There's a snowman contest on
Saturday!" said Henry.
"Snowman contest!" said Henry's
father. He wiped some paint
on his ears. "Wow!"

"Can we go?" asked Henry.

"Sure!" said Henry's father.

He wiped some paint on his elbow.

Henry looked at his father.

Henry looked at the chair.

"Dad, I think that chair has been painting *you*," said Henry.

Henry's dad looked at himself
in an old mirror.

He had green hair, a green nose,
a green mustache, a green chin,
green ears, and a green elbow.

Henry's dad looked at Henry.

He said, "You should see me
when I paint a *house!*"

At the Park

On Saturday, Henry and
Henry's father and
Henry's big dog Mudge
went to the park.
There were many people there.

All of the people had things.
They had shovels and spoons.
They had hats and shoes.

They had rocks and carrots
and marbles and broccoli.
"Broccoli?" said Henry
to his father.

And, of course, they all had dogs.
"It looks more like a
wagging contest to me,"
said Henry's father.
Mudge wagged and wagged.

Henry and his dad had already
made their snowman plan.
They looked at each other.
They shook hands.
"Good luck, break a leg,
and don't let the bedbugs bite,"
said Henry's father.
And they got to work.

While Henry and his father built
their snowman, Mudge visited.
He visited a poodle.

He visited a husky.

He visited a dachshund

who didn't want to visit him.

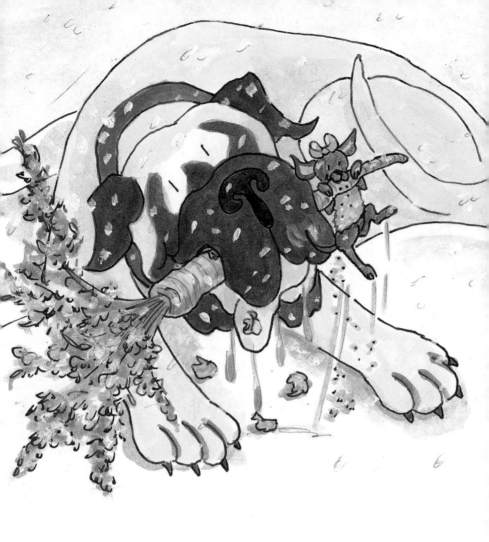

Then he found a carrot to
chew on.

A Chihuahua helped him chew it.

Mudge finished his half first.

It looked like the Chihuahua
might finish hers
sometime in July.
Mudge wagged and
gave her a kiss.

Snow Aliens

By 3:00 all of the snowmen
were ready for the judges.
Henry and his father
looked around the park.

There were snowpeople.

There were snowcats.

There were snowdogs.

There were snow aliens.

And one person had built
a snow Abraham Lincoln.
"Wow!" said Henry.

The judges walked all around.

Henry was feeling nervous.

He held Mudge's collar.

Holding Mudge's collar

always helped when

Henry was nervous.

"I hope they like ours,"
Henry said.
"Me too," said Henry's dad,
holding Mudge's collar
on the other side.

Finally the judges arrived.

They looked carefully at the

snowman Henry and his father

had built.

They looked at the front.

They looked at the back.

They looked all around.

Finally one of them asked,

"What is it?"

"It's my dad when he's painting

a chair," said Henry.

The judges looked again
and laughed and laughed.
Mudge wagged and drooled
on their boots.

When the winners were
announced, first place went
to Abraham Lincoln.
Second place went to a
snow leopard.

And third place went to
the snowman with paint
in his mustache.
"Yay!" yelled Henry.
Henry and Henry's father
proudly looked at their prizes.

One was a purple ribbon.

It said THIRD PLACE WINNER,

MOST ORIGINAL SNOWMAN.

And the other prize was

a big box of snowman cookies.

"I sure am glad you're a
messy painter, Dad,"
said Henry.
"I'm an even messier *eater*,"
said Henry's father.

39

And he and Henry
and Henry's big dog Mudge
took their prizes home and
made a wonderful cookie mess.